POKÉMON

TRAINER ACTIVITY BOOK: JOURNEY TO THE KALOS REGION

TRAINER ACTIVITY BOOK: JOURNEY TO THE KALOS REGION

$12.99 USA
$15.50 CAN

The Pokémon Company
INTERNATIONAL

Publisher: Heather Dalgleish
Publishing Manager: Amy Levenson
Writer: Lawrence Neves
Editor: Wolfgang Baur
Art Director: Eric Medalle
Cover Designer: Chris Franc
Merchandise Development Director: Phaedra Long
Merchandise Development: Hank Woon
Project Manager: Emily Luty

The Pokémon Company International
333 108th Avenue NE, Suite 1900
Bellevue, WA 98004

Printed in Guangdong, China.

This book was produced by Walter Foster Publishing, a division of Quarto Publishing Group USA Inc.

ISBN: 978-1-60438-182-5

Special thanks to my son Nicholas Neves for all his help and encouragement. That kid knows his Pokémon!

POKÉMON™
TRAINER ACTIVITY BOOK:
JOURNEY TO THE KALOS REGION

TABLE OF CONTENTS

CENTRAL KALOS

Welcome to the Kalos region, Pokémon fans! Get ready, get set, and start your training to become a specialist in the types of Pokémon that populate the Central, Coastal, and Mountain subregions of Kalos! You'll need a sharp eye, keen wit, and lots of Pokémon smarts to make it through–but we know you can do it! Let's get started with the Pokémon of the Central subregion of Kalos!

FILL OUT THE INFORMATION CARD ON PANGORO!

Pangoro is one of the many Pokémon of the Central subregion. Let's start by seeing how much information you can fill out about this awesome Pokémon!

Pangoro

Height: _____

Weight: _____

Type(s): _____ lbs.

Weaknesses: _____

Unevolved Form: _____

Turn to page 91 for the answers.

WHICH FURFROU IS WHICH?

Furfrou: Trimming its fluffy fur into many different styles makes it both fancier and faster. There are several other trims, but see if you can match the correct Furfrou to the correct trim!

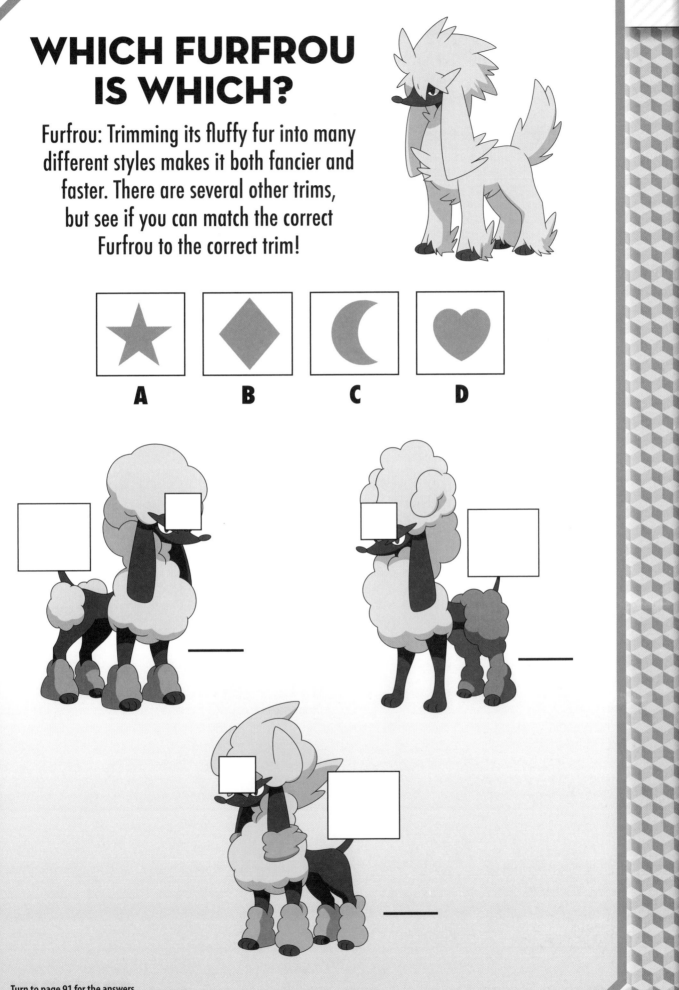

A   B   C   D

Turn to page 91 for the answers.

VIVILLON CROSSWORD

DOWN

1. Vivillon starts out as this Pokémon
2. Vivillon's second type
5. The first Evolution of Vivillon
8. Vivillon is weak against this type

ACROSS

1. _____ Dust is one of Vivillon's Abilities
3. Spewpa lives hidden within _____ shadows
4. Compound _____ is Vivillon's other Ability
6. Vivillon with many different _____ are found all over the world
7. One of Vivillon's types
9. This type isn't very effective against Vivillon

Turn to page 91 for the answers.

WORD SEARCH

Espurr is a Psychic-type Pokémon that is looking for all of its Pokémon friends from the Central subregion of Kalos. Can you help it find the following Pokémon?

```
P V V X V G G M Z O G O A T L W Z G Q A T F L
H U Z R R O Y B R R Z X F L E T C H L I N G I L I
G U N B W B H F W A O Y G C K B R U Q O É J F A T
N K H D S S E A Z H B U N N E L B Y W J F V O B L
I É J S P T I K P B C N Z I I K C A P V S Z F É E
É C Q T T M O L K N Z H H O F F G I Y M C S L B O
U Y J E Q M E T I C H L L A S K I D D O A L O É F
D V O U Y D D K U O O C A Z É E O V F T T G R G U
J L L C I K E S C H E S P I N R P I R N T F G D R
F K N P A N I P E D U Z V U O A B S O I E Z E O F
N H D U N Y W E E B U Q U G F K E K A L R P S F R
O D V E U D K W N O Q A N P Q Q W B K B B N A L O
A J F L C D P P K N M A J W C É W O I C U X C Z U
C P G M U V X A T C P J U V E W P M E Z G M J S F
É G M Q G T P L V I V I L L O N K C P Y R O A R X
```

BUNNELBY · CHESPIN · DELPHOX · FENNEKIN · FLABÉBÉ · FLETCHLING · FLOETTE

FLORGES · FROAKIE · FURFROU · GOGOAT · LITLEO · PANGORO

PYROAR · SCATTERBUG · SKIDDO · SPEWPA · VIVILLON

Turn to page 91 for the answers.

GUESS THE EVOLUTION

These three Pokémon are all in the same Evolution chain.
Can you guess the order?
Let's see if you know your Kalos Pokémon!

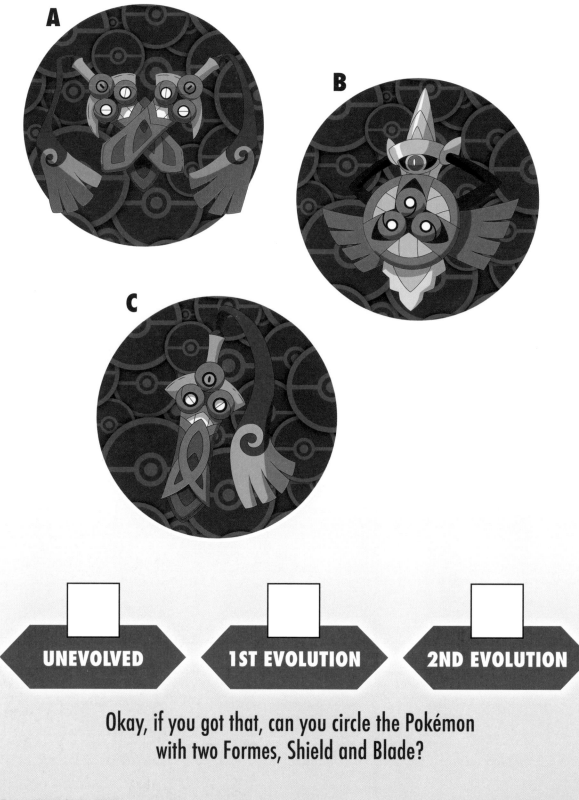

A

B

C

| UNEVOLVED | 1ST EVOLUTION | 2ND EVOLUTION |

Okay, if you got that, can you circle the Pokémon
with two Formes, Shield and Blade?

Turn to page 91 for the answers.

DOTS WHAT I'M TALKING ABOUT

Finding Pokémon isn't always about the visuals. Sometimes you have to rely on your instincts and maybe a brief glimpse of your Pokémon. Take a close look at the picture below and see if you can piece together the Kalos Pokémon we're looking for!

CLUE 1:
It's a Grass type

CLUE 2:
It can create energy via photosynthesis

CLUE 3:
It can eventually evolve into Gogoat

Turn to page 91 for the answer.

SEEK AND FIND

We've lost count of the different types of Central subregion Pokémon in Kalos. But wait—if you really know the Pokémon of this subregion, pick out at least two more Pokémon that are the exact same type as Gogoat. Types matter, Pokémon Specialists!

Turn to page 91 for the answers.

WORD SCRAMBLE

Slurpuff needs help identifying another Pokémon.
Below are clues with one letter removed.
Fill in the puzzle, then unscramble the letters
to find the missing Pokémon.

1. It ☐oves to snack on sweets.

2. It's kno☐n as the Cotton
Candy Pokémon.

3. It's a Fai☐y-type Pokémon.

4. It's got an e☐tra-fluffy exterior.

5. It's weak against ☐teel and Poison types.

6. Its sugary eating habits have made its white
fur sweet and sticky, just l☐ke cotton candy.

7. It has one Evolut☐on stage.

☐ ☐ ☐ ☐ ☐ ☐ ☐
1. 2. 3. 4. 5. 6. 7.

?

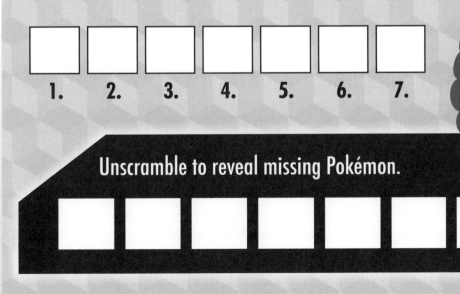

Unscramble to reveal missing Pokémon.

☐ ☐ ☐ ☐ ☐ ☐ ☐

Turn to page 91 for the answers.

FIND THE DIFFERENCE

So far, so good, Kalos Specialist! Let's try to strengthen our visual skills so that we can identify Kalos Pokémon at a glance. Below are four Pancham-but only one is the real Pancham! Look for subtle differences in colors, appendages, or expressions. Find the real Pancham!

A

B

C

D

Turn to page 91 for the answer.

CRYPTO GRAPHICS

Professional Kalos Pokémon Specialists have been leaving coded messages all over the Central subregion of Kalos looking for other specialists to talk to. But they've been replacing letters with Pokémon so that only the top specialists can decode their messages.

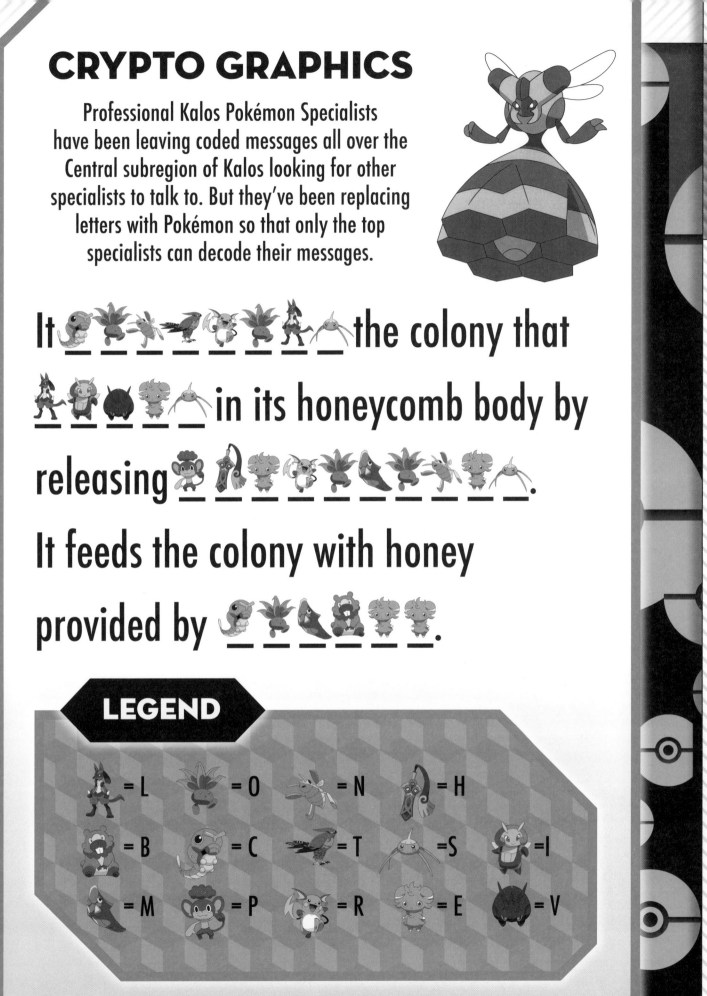

It _____ the colony that _____ in its honeycomb body by releasing _____. It feeds the colony with honey provided by _____.

LEGEND

= L	= O	= N	= H
= B	= C	= T	= S	= I
= M	= P	= R	= E	= V

Turn to page 92 for the answers.

Certificate of Completion

This is to certify that

_____

has achieved the rank of Pokémon Specialist of the Central subregion of Kalos.

FURFROU

PANCHAM

VIVILLON

ESPURR

SKIDDO

HONEDGE

SLURPUFF

Issued this _____ day of

_____, 20__

COASTAL KALOS

As we move out of the Central subregion and down to the shore,
the Pokémon change—and a good Pokémon Specialist knows what lives where.
Get on some sunscreen, it's time to visit the Coastal subregion!

FINISH THE POKÉMON

The sea salt tends to wash colors out in the Coastal subregion of Kalos.
Help us to bring some life back to Skrelp! Color this Pokémon and we'll
see if you know your Kalos Pokémon as well as we know you do!

Turn to page 92 for the answer.

POKÉMON FINDER

You can spot Coastal subregion
Pokémon a mile away–but can
you spot them a mile a wave?

RULES: Hidden among these waves are ten Pokémon.
Take a pen, pencil, or marker and throw your Poké Ball at ten squares.
See if you can catch ten Coastal subregion Pokémon!

LEGEND

0-3 Catches: You can ride the waves with the best of them!
4-7 Catches: You are one with the water!
8-10 Catches: You "sea" better than most Trainers!

Turn to page 92 for the answers.

19

POKÉMON SUDOKU

Part of being a great Pokémon Specialist is knowing how your Pokémon interact with each other. Inkay wants to confuse you as you try to identify your Pokémon. See if you can avoid getting hypnotized by Inkay's lights and complete this Sudoku puzzle.

			3		7	5	4	
		8			6	9	2	
	2	3			8			
	5	6						
		7		1		3		
						8		9
			8			1		6
	8	5	2			4		
	7	4	5		3			

The spots on Inkay's body emit a flashing light. This light confuses its opponents, giving it a chance to escape.

Turn to page 92 for the answers.

20

RHYHORN RACING

Rhyhorn are entered in races, and later on you'll meet a Trainer whose mom was a Rhyhorn racing champion. See if you can get Rhyhorn from the starting line to the finish line without any false moves!

FINISH

START

Turn to page 92 for the answer.

WHAT'S IN THE POKÉ BALL?

During your adventures in Kalos, you might find a stray
Poké Ball that a Trainer left behind at a Pokémon Center.
The Trainer left some notes about the Pokémon inside the Poké Ball,
but forgot to write down the Pokémon's name! See if you can
guess which Pokémon is in the ball, just from the clues!

SCORING

See how fast you can figure out what's in the Poké Ball.
Score is based on how many clues you use.
1-3 Clues: You really know your Kalos Coastal subregion Pokémon!
4-7 Clues: You deserve this! You're doing well for a
Pokémon Specialist!
8-9 Clues: You'd be great on anyone's Pokémon Team!

CLUE 1:
It's an Electric- and
Normal-type Pokémon

CLUE 2:
It's the
Generator Pokémon

CLUE 3:
It has the Dry Skin Ability

Turn to page 92 for the answer.

BEACH SCRAWL

While traveling along the coast of Kalos, you notice that someone has scrawled the names of Pokémon in the sand. Could these clues be the names of Pokémon you're searching for? Can you decipher these sandy scrawls and uncover which Pokémon they refer to?

AH MA OR AH

DHRAG ALJ

SIL VEE UN

HOWL OO CHA

NK

BY NAK EL

KLAWN CHAIR

TIE WRUNT

Turn to page 92 for the answers.

23

PIECE OF MINE

Here's a test to see if you can spot the Pokémon from the Coastal subregion–even if all you get is a glimpse of part of them! Match the Pokémon pieces to their Pokémon.

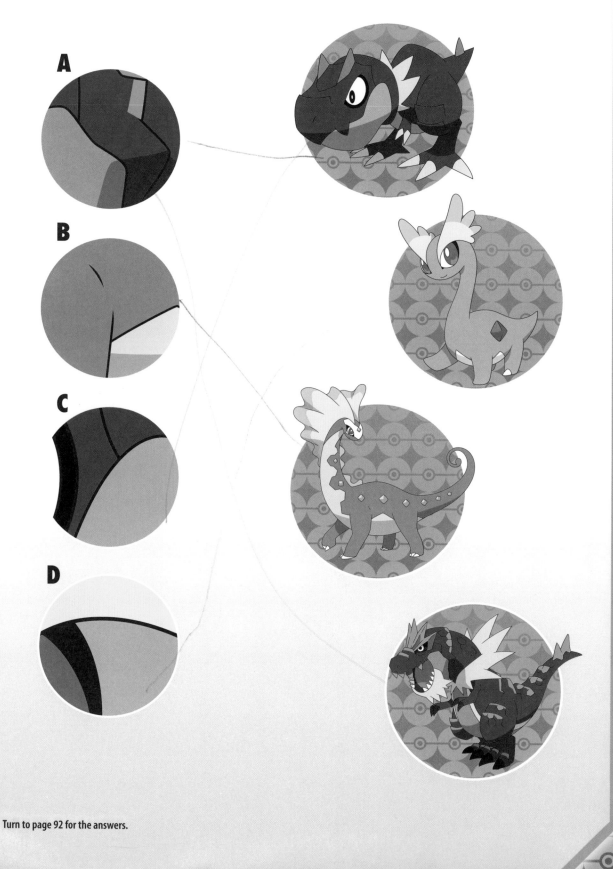

A

B

C

D

Turn to page 92 for the answers.

POKÉMON ACROSTICS

Let's see how much you know about the Coastal subregion of Kalos, and the Pokémon that live there. Play this game with one, two, or three players!

RULES

Pick a Pokémon name. Write that name in a column. If you picked Dragalge, you should have a puzzle that looks like this. Now, try to spell the longest word you can with the letters in each row. For example, starting with the first row, try to spell a word that starts with D, but very long, like DIMINISHING. You can only make one word per row, but you get one point for each letter used. Try for the longest word you know!

BONUS

Time the game and see how many words you can come up with in two minutes.

D _____

R _____

A _____

G _____

A _____

L _____

G _____

E _____

POKÉMON NAME GAME

Speed is essential with slippery Coastal subregion Pokémon. Identifying your Pokémon before they disappear into the depths of a body of water is very important. Here's a one-, two-, or multi-player word game that tests how quick you are at identifying Pokémon.

Clauncher

1. Her
2. Launch
3. Lunch
4. Haul
5. Lance
6. Hare
7. Luna
8. Real
9. Run
10. Hue
11. Clue

RULES

You and a friend pick out a Kalos Pokémon, like Clauncher. Each of you then writes that Pokémon down on a piece of paper. Now, come up with as many words as you can using the letters from that Pokémon name within a two-minute time limit. The player with the most words after two minutes wins.

WORD SEARCH

The Psychic- and Dark-type Malamar is trying to remember a great number of Coastal subregion Pokémon. Help it by finding the Pokémon listed below.

```
J D T N B F H F N N K T D Q Z E C T K I N K A Y
G O L E T T J B V O X W Z Z F B I N A C L E M O
J S A W C J T Y R A N T R U M M I C P B A O A T
F Q N C S D Z T Y R U N T B P J J S P C B E L Q
D D B O Y O I V K T R Z J L K X F U A L I N A X
Y A H Z X K H V D T Z O E C K J N N H A V U M H
H E L I O L I S K E I R E S S A J I C U E K A P
P J P N E B N W U Q K L J Y T G D L O N L R R H
K I M V F Z G D N S I G E L A W Y W H C C T M X
T D Y L Y X Q H U T Q G T V T P G I S H L J V A
S I G I L Y P H P E L R A E M U P U B E A R V M
R Q J L P J F O X A V H Y O Y M R C T R W B U A
E G R C I E I Y G A C G D N S O T Y B V I P B U
Z F I D M L P A S U R F V Y R Y T O O Y T T W R
O L S I E R R V L U K Q Q U B D B M S I Z M X A
N L Y H V D A W J T S B A R B A R A C L E S R J
N E H B I M A N T M N E L Y D S D C S T R I S M
M R N C D H W A E S O I N G H I L T V W J I G B
```

INKAY   MALAMAR   BINACLE   BARBARACLE   SKRELP   DRAGALGE   CLAUNCHER

CLAWITZER   HELIOPTILE   HELIOLISK   TYRUNT   TYRANTRUM   AMAURA

AURORUS   SYLVEON   HAWLUCHA   SIGILYPH   GOLETT

Turn to page 92 for the answers.

Certificate of Completion

This is to certify that

_____

has achieved the rank of Pokémon Specialist of the Coastal subregion of Kalos.

HELIOPTILE

INKAY

SKRELP

TYRUNT

AMAURA

SYLVEON

CLAUNCHER

Issued this _____ day of

_____, 20___

MOUNTAIN KALOS

Far above the Coastal and Central portions of Kalos
are its snow-capped mountains! It's time to explore the
Pokémon of this subregion: what do you think you'll find?

WORD SCRAMBLE

Not all Pokémon in the Mountain subregion of Kalos are easy to understand. You sometimes have to make an effort to decipher what they're trying to tell you. Pumpkaboo is trying to tell you something about itself. See if you can decipher what it's trying to say by taking the highlighted letter from each clue and reassembling them into the words below!

1. Ghost- and Grass-type Pokémon, and its name rhymes with bump
AHNPTMPU _ _ ☐ ☐ ☐ _ _ _

2. Goomy's first evolved form
OLGIGOS _ ☐ _ _ _ ☐ _

3. Pumpkaboo's evolved form
GSGROUEIT _ _ ☐ ☐ _ _ _ _ ☐

4. A Legendary Pokémon in Kalos
LLVETYA _ _ _ _ _ _ ☐

5. Pumpkaboo's type
THOGS/SARGS _ _ _ ☐ _ / _ ☐ _ _ ☐

6. When cracks in its body form, it uses freezing air to patch itself up with new ice.
MEERGITB _ ☐ _ _ _ _ _ ☐

7. A Water-type Pokémon with a name that is pronounced BASS-kyoo-lin
NILUCSAB _ _ ☐ ☐ _ _ _ ☐

---

1. ☐☐☐ 2. ☐☐ 3. ☐☐☐ 4. ☐ 5. ☐☐☐ 6. ☐☐ 7. ☐☐☐

ANSWER

Unscramble to reveal the message.

The _ _ _ _ _ _ _ _ _ _ Pumpkaboo tends to get _ _ _ _ _ _ _ _ _ as darkness falls.

Turn to page 92 for the answers.

FIND THE DIFFERENCE

A good Kalos Pokémon Specialist knows when and how to spot a fake. Some of these Pokémon have a slight change – shape, appendages, color – and it's up to you and your sleuthing skills to find out which one is the real Pokémon!

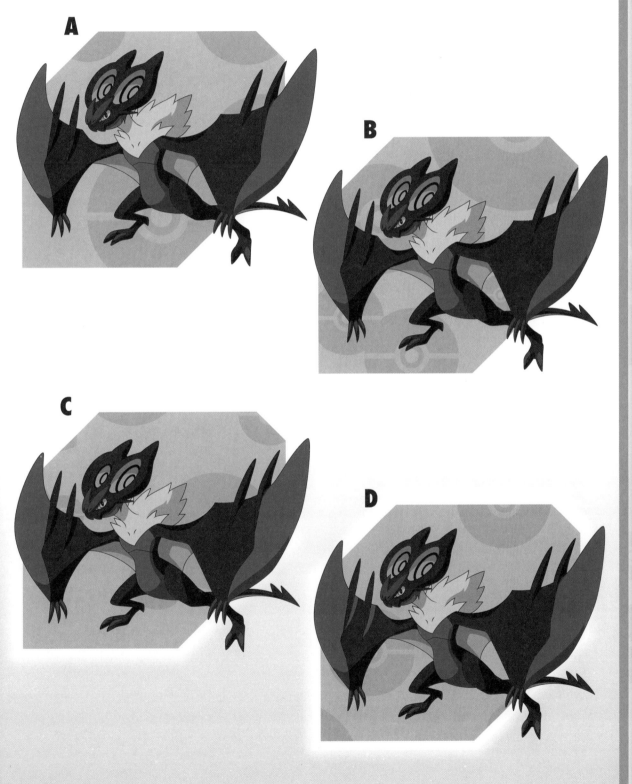

A

B

C

D

Turn to page 93 for the answer.

WHODUNNIT?

Rotom is trying to figure out who broke the refrigerator in the hall. Don't worry–Rotom can fix it, but it wants to know who's responsible. See if you can use these clues to find out who Rotom can blame. Maybe it's another Forme of Rotom?

1. One of its types is Fairy.
2. This Pokémon does not evolve.
3. It's weak against Fire and Ground types.
4. If you want to keep valuables locked up tight, give the key to this Pokémon.
5. It loves to collect keys and will guard its collection with all its might.

1. It loves sparkly things. It seeks treasures in caves and hoards the loot in its nest.
2. It used to be a Gible.
3. It is a Dragon- and Ground-type Pokémon.
4. Its second Evolution can Mega-Evolve.
5. It is weak against Ice, Dragon, Fairy, Water, and Grass types.

1. Live in lightless caves and communicate with ultrasonic waves emitted from their ears.
2. Its ultrasonic waves can make a strong man dizzy.
3. It's a dual-type Pokémon.
4. This Pokémon and its Evolution is seen for the first time in Kalos.
5. One of its types is Dragon.

Have you guessed which three Pokémon Rotom suspects? Good! The Pokémon that Rotom is looking for has the Prankster Ability! Have you guessed who it is yet?

Turn to page 93 for the answers.

A PUZZLE OF POKÉMON

Let's see if your identification skills have improved, Kalos Specialist!
Draw a line from the puzzle pieces to the missing spots in the puzzle.
Be careful! A wrong move might cost you your certificate!

A

B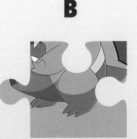

C

Turn to page 93 for the answers.

DOTS WHAT I'M TALKING ABOUT

Quick! Can you spot Pokémon as easily in a mountain cave as on shimmering coastline? Let's test your sighting skills in the Mountain subregion of Kalos. See if you can use the clues to identify this Pokémon.

CLUE 1:
Has two Forms that are constantly fighting.

CLUE 2:
Does not evolve.

CLUE 3:
Its two Forms are rarely found in the same place.

If you guessed it in:
1 Clue: Your training is nearly complete!
2 Clues: You are really filling out your Pokédex!
3 Clues: I want you on my team!

Turn to page 93 for the answer.

MATCH THE TYPE

Okay, you may know your Kalos Pokémon—but do you know their types? See if you can match up the types to the Pokémon they belong to.

DRAGON

FLYING | PSYCHIC

GHOST | DRAGON

GHOST | GRASS

ICE

WATER | ICE

Turn to page 93 for the answers.

WHAT'S IN THE POKÉ BALL?

Another Trainer must have been really distracted because someone dropped a Poké Ball, and all the notes about the Pokémon inside! See if you can help return this Pokémon to its Trainer by first correctly identifying what it is by the notes!

1. Sings in an eerie voice
2. It's a dual type—and one of them is Grass
3. Its song echoes through town on nights during the new moon
4. It was a Pumpkaboo in the past
5. Anyone who hears its song feels woe
6. It weighs 27.6 lbs.
7. It is the Pumpkin Pokémon
8. Its name rhymes with heist

SCORING

See how fast you can figure out what's in the Poké Ball.
Score is based on how many clues you use.
1-3 Clues: You really know your Mountain subregion Pokémon!
4-6 Clues: You deserve this! You're doing well for a Pokémon Specialist!
7-8 Clues: You'd be great on anyone's Pokémon Team!

Turn to page 93 for the answer.

MMMMMMMM...POKÉMON

See if you can help Magneton find out what these Mountain subregion Pokémon are mucking on about! They're manic, they're mobile, and they're mysterious. Be careful—the Pokémon in here all start with the same letter, except for one!

MOUNTAIN KALOS

DOWN

1. Their huge twin tusks are formed of ice.

3. When it goes on a rampage it causes so much damage to the landscape that maps have to be updated.

4. They hunt in packs and work together to take down an opponent.

5. Some people believe that if you see them at night, bad luck will follow.

ACROSS

2. Several Magnemite link together to form a single one of these.

4. The final Evolution of 7 ACROSS.

6. Because of the brutal experiments it was part of, it is extremely savage and dangerous.

7. From the units at its sides, it generates an antigravity field to keep itself afloat.

8. It has several Formes, all mechanical variations. This one looks like it could cut some grass if needed.

9. Its body is so hot that its brittle shell sometimes bursts into flame, giving off waves of intense heat.

Turn to page 93 for the answers.

POKÉMON FINDER

Before you go mountain climbing, you need to hone your Specialist skills! See if you can find mountain Pokémon hidden behind these rocks. Take a pen, pencil, or marker and mark off ten spots. See if you can catch ten Pokémon from the Mountain subregion of Kalos!

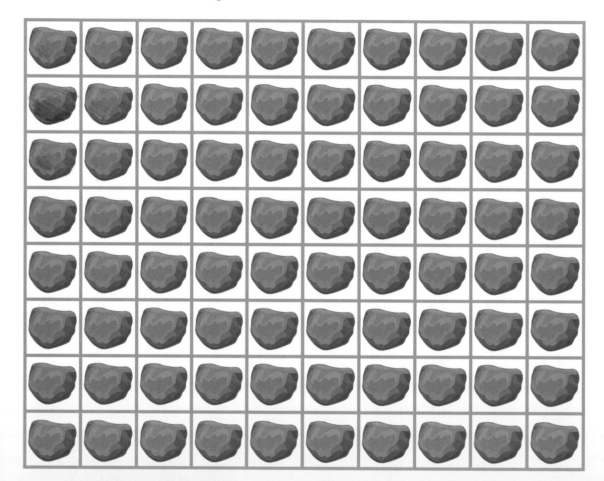

LEGEND

0-3 Catches: You rock with the best of them!

4-7 Catches: You are one with the mountains!

8-10 Catches: You're "boulder" than most Trainers!

Turn to page 93 for the answers.

WORD SEARCH

The Dark-type Pokémon Zorua wants to find where some of the Pokémon in the Mountain subregion of Kalos went. Help it find the rest of its friends in the puzzle below.

```
A I X M H D J Y P T R P S V X N H M P E E Z
N M K F T K L E F K I H B O F Y Z A H I I I
S T Q W Z F I Z S P D A J S G Y O G V D U I
R B B Q O F J V T U B N V E Z S R O H I M M
F B A S C U L I N M U T D N K N O I V E R N
Q G V V A I G N R P X U C K P R A M G P X E
G I W T Q S A P C K I M G O O D R A O N Z D
O N N R H L R G R A W P Y T W X K L U B V M
O N B E B I C H A B W J O Q Z O Z M R E G W
M O N V X G H O V O C N C N E F V W G R J V
Y J T E A G O Y H O I J N Y C R P L E G T K
O A R N R O M U Q E X V S Z N E O Q I M E I
Y F I A T O P E D H O N F W N K L J S I T C
F K E N A X N Y B K N Y C U Q F L B T T I Q
Z P W T C U B C H O O X U N B U D C D E J M
```

BASCULIN   BERGMITE   CUBCHOO   DEINO   GARCHOMP   GOODRA

GOOMY   GOURGEIST   KLEFKI   NOIVERN   PHANTUMP   PUMPKABOO

SLIGGOO   TREVENANT   ZOROARK

Turn to page 93 for the answers.

Certificate of Completion

This is to certify that

_____

has achieved the rank of Pokémon Specialist of the Mountain subregion of Kalos.

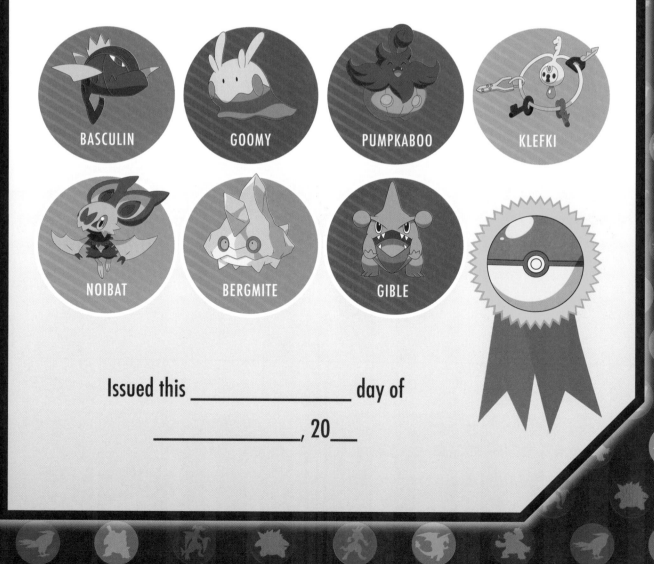

BASCULIN · GOOMY · PUMPKABOO · KLEFKI

NOIBAT · BERGMITE · GIBLE

Issued this _____ day of

_____, 20___

TRAVELING PARTY

Although you can travel through Kalos alone, most Trainers benefit from having their friends along. Meet some of the people Ash has met so far, and the Pokémon they travel with.

COMPLETE THE TRAINER

So you've passed all the Specialist Training to become an expert in the Central, Coastal, and Mountain subregions of Kalos. Now let's see if you know the people you'll meet on your journey. The first is the most famous Trainer around—Ash Ketchum! See if you can fill in the colors that Ash wears in Kalos—and no peeking at the next page!

Turn to page 93 for the answer.

TRAVELING PARTY

WHO'S YOUR FRIEND?

Ash is eager to collect badges in Kalos. He won't let anything slow him down—and he also won't go it alone. See if you recognize the first two Kalos Pokémon that Ash captures from the group below.

Turn to page 93 for the answers.

43

A PUZZLE OF POKÉMON

Let's see if your identification skills have improved, Kalos Specialist!
Draw a line from the puzzle pieces to the missing spots in the puzzle.
Be careful! A wrong move might cost you your certificate!

A

B

C

Turn to page 94 for the answers.

WALL SCRAWL

Ash left clues about Pokémon he hopes to see in Kalos. Some of them are Pokémon he wants to catch, and some he wants to battle. To keep his plans secret, he's coded the Pokémon so only he can read the list. See if you can decipher the Pokémon he's after!

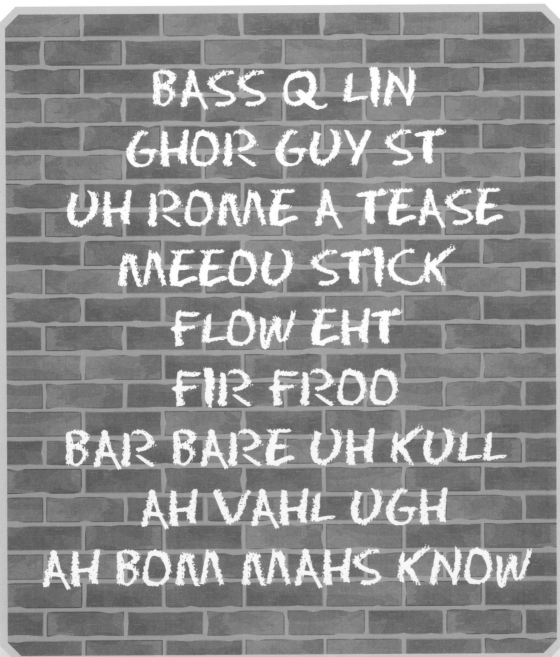

BASS Q LIN

GHOR GUY ST

UH ROME A TEASE

MEEOU STICK

FLOW EHT

FIR FROO

BAR BARE UH KULL

AH VAHL UGH

AH BOM MAHS KNOW

Turn to page 94 for the answers.

POKÉMON FINDER

We know Ash can spot Pokémon with ease. Can you? Using a marker, pen, or pencil, mark off ten spots. See if you can spot ten Pokémon!

LEGEND

0-3 Catches: You can join our team any time!

4-7 Catches: You have a keen eye and great aim!

8-10 Catches: Maybe you should head up your own team?

Turn to page 94 for the answers.

ODD POKÉMON OUT!

Ash's Froakie is a Water type. See if you can recognize other Water-type Pokémon that Froakie might battle during Ash's travels in the Kalos region. But wait, are you sure that all of these Pokémon are only Water types? Let's see if you know which Pokémon are dual types and which subregion they can be found in.

Turn to page 94 for the answers.

POKÉMON NAME GAME

Identifying your Pokémon before they disappear is very important to a Trainer. Here's a one-, two-, or multi-player word game that tests how quick you are at identifying Pokémon.

RULES

You and a friend pick out a Kalos Pokémon, like Fletchling. Each of you then writes that Pokémon's name down on a piece of paper. Now, come up with as many words as you can with the letters from that Pokémon name within a two-minute time limit. The player with the most words after two minutes win.

Fletchling

1. Fetch
2. Let
3. Fling
4. Line
5. Glint
6. Lift
7. Get
8. Net
9. Hit
10. Fit
11. Tile

MATCH THE MOVE

There's no really big secrets to being a Trainer—
it just takes skill and a sense of what your Pokémon are capable of!
How well do you know your Pokémon? See if you can match the
Pokémon on the left to the moves on the right!

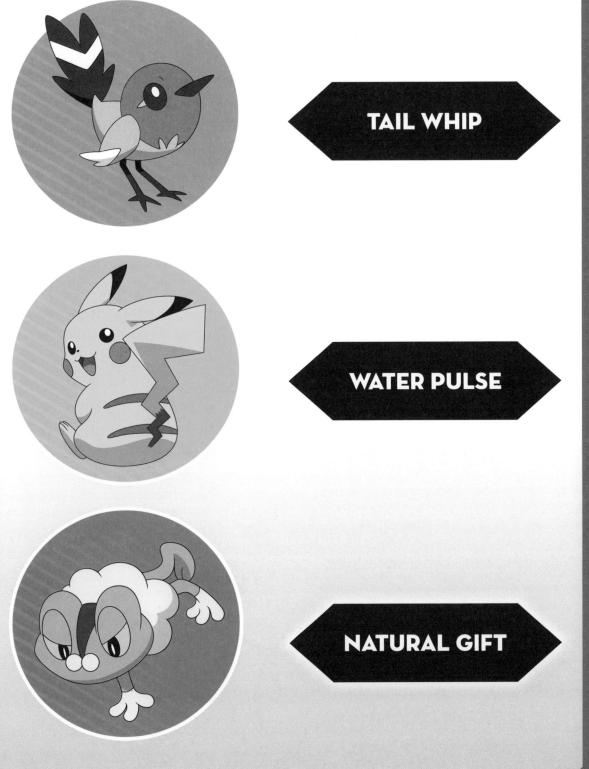

TAIL WHIP

WATER PULSE

NATURAL GIFT

Turn to page 94 for the answers.

KNOWLEDGE BASE

Here are some tough questions that only a Trainer would know.
See if you can keep up!

1. What is the name of the professor in Kalos?

2. Where does Ash visit first, Lumiose City or Santalune Gym?

3. What Pokémon does Team Rocket catch first, Inkay or Pumpkaboo?

4. True or False: Bonnie is a Trainer.

5. Serena's mother used to be an expert _____ Racer.

6. Team Rocket is hypnotized by _____.

7. Snorlax's snoring greatly affects the people of _____ Town.

8. On the way to the Battle Chateau, Ash and friends meet the brothers _____ and _____.

9. Viola is a _____-type Trainer.

10. The Pokémon Smuggler's name is _____.

Turn to page 94 for the answers.

EVOLUTION REVOLUTION

Can you match the Pokémon with their evolved forms? Put these Pokémon in the correct order from just-hatched to final evolved form!

A

B

C

D

1ST EVOLUTION

2ND EVOLUTION

1ST EVOLUTION

2ND EVOLUTION

Turn to page 94 for the answers.

SEEK AND FIND

Identifying Hawlucha in a group is tough—this Pokémon is quick, powerful, and colorful. Identify Hawlucha in this group, and then pick out all of the other types that match Hawlucha's first type. Ash is depending on your skill and expertise, Pokémon Specialist!

Turn to page 94 for the answers.

CLEMONT

Clemont is a true handyman—or at least he fancies himself one.
His Clemontic Gear saves Ash a couple of times—
which is why Ash is glad to have him around!

COMPLETE THE TRAINER

So you've passed all the Specialist Training to become an expert in the Central, Coastal, and Mountain subregions of Kalos. Now let's see if you know the people you'll meet on your journey. Next up is the master inventor and tinkerer, Clemont! See if you can fill in the colors that Clemont wears—and no peeking at the next page!

Turn to page 94 for the answer.

CLEMONT

WHO'S YOUR FRIEND?

Clemont isn't very athletic, but he is very smart.
He relies on his Pokémon to help him get through the day in Kalos.
See if you can identify Pokémon that Clemont has captured!

Turn to page 94 for the answers.

A PUZZLE OF POKÉMON

Let's see if your identification skills have improved, Kalos Specialist!
Draw a line from the puzzle pieces to the missing spots in the puzzle.
Be careful! A wrong move might cost you!

A

B

C

Turn to page 94 for the answers.

WALL SCRAWL

Clemont is pretty forgetful—most brilliant people are! He's scrawled the names of different Pokémon he might have plans to invent items for around the lab. See if you can help him figure out which Pokémon he had on his radar.

GHO GHO T

EZPR

HO NEJ

S P ON

HAR EEYAM AH

GI GAL ETH

CRI OGG UN AL

ZO REW AH

MYENSH OW

MAL M R

BUHN LB

Turn to page 95 for the answers.

POKÉMON FINDER

Can you help Clemont find more Pokémon? He has plans...plans that involve more Pokémon! Using a marker, pen, or pencil, mark off ten spots where you would throw Poké Balls. See if you can find ten more Pokémon to help out Clemont!

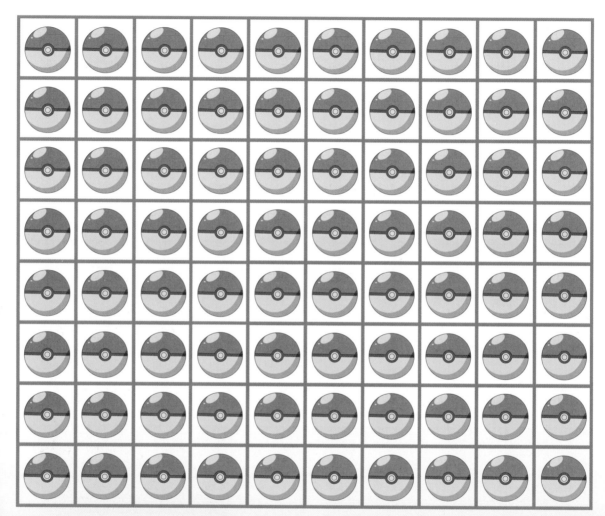

LEGEND

0-3 Catches: You can join our team any time!

4-7 Catches: You have a keen eye and great aim!

8-10 Catches: Maybe you should head up your own team?

Turn to page 95 for the answers.

ODD POKÉMON OUT

So you know your Pokémon by sight, but can you really hang with Trainers and sort out the Pokémon that stand out in a crowd?

Rules: For this test, we're going to show you some different Pokémon. One of these doesn't belong in the group, but which one? And what is the group? We'll give you three clues. You score yourself by how many clues you used!

CLUE 1:
They make a great start

CLUE 2:
Trainers snatch them up right away

CLUE 3:
One comes later

SCORING

1 Clue: You know your Pokémon well!
2 Clues: You're doing well for a Specialist!
3 Clues: Join our team!

Turn to page 95 for the answers.

POKÉMON NAME GAME

Identifying your Pokémon before they disappear is very important to a Trainer. Here's a one-, two-, or multi-player word game that tests how quick you are with your Pokémon?

RULES

You and a friend pick out a Kalos Pokémon, like Bunnelby. Each of you then writes that Pokémon's name down on a piece of paper. Now, come up with as many words as you can with the letters from that Pokémon name within a two-minute time limit. The player with the most words after two minutes wins.

Bunnelby

1. Blub
2. Buy
3. Bye
4. Bun
5. Blue
6. Lune
7. Nubbly

MATCH THE MOVE

Clemont's Pokémon, Bunnelby and Chespin, might battle some Pokémon in Kalos with the same type. Bunnelby is a Normal-type Pokémon, and so is Lickitung. Chespin is a Grass type and so is Bellossom. But do you know what moves they each can use in battle? See if you can match the Pokémon on the left to the moves on the right!

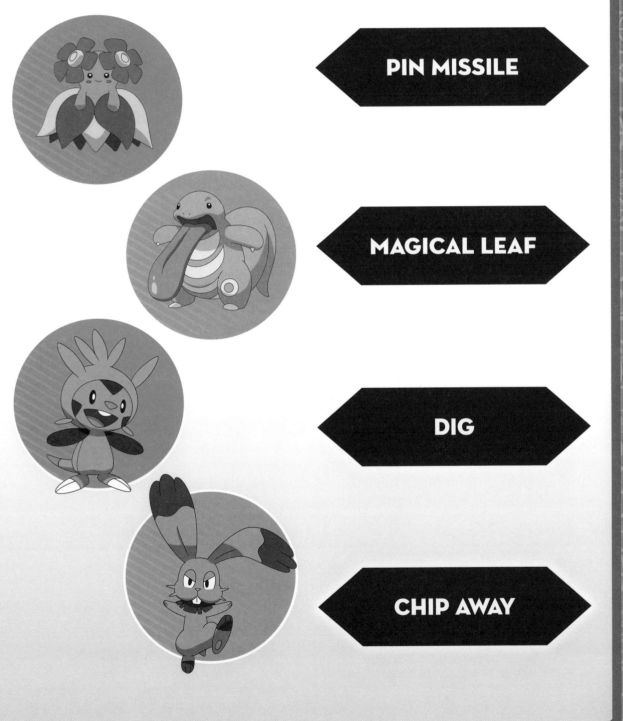

PIN MISSILE

MAGICAL LEAF

DIG

CHIP AWAY

Turn to page 95 for the answers.

CLEMONT

KNOWLEDGE BASE

Here are some tough questions that only a Trainer would know.
See if you can keep up!

1. Serena chooses this as her first partner Pokémon.

2. He's a popular Furfrou Groomer.

3. True or false: Bonnie is Clemont's cousin.

4. Ash and friends discover a Magikarp in this special color.

5. Serena's new hair style attracts this Pokémon.

6. Froakie uses these, but it is not a move.

7. True or false: Ash is previously acquainted with Serena.

8. The first Mega-Evolved Pokémon that Ash and friends meet is

_____.

9. Ash scales a rock-climbing wall in this gym.

Turn to page 95 for the answers.

CLEMONT

EVOLUTION REVOLUTION

Can you match the Pokémon with their evolved forms? Put these Pokémon in the correct order from freshly hatched to final evolved form!

A

B

C

[ ]

1ST EVOLUTION

[ ]

1ST EVOLUTION

[ ]

2ND EVOLUTION

Turn to page 95 for the answers.

CLEMONT

TYPE CAST

Clemont sends Bunnelby out so he can battle and catch Dedenne for his sister. But is Dedenne only an Electric type or is it a dual-type Pokémon? Can you identify it and these other Kalos Pokémon. Remember, types are extremely important in battle. See if you can match Pokémon on the left with their type on the right!

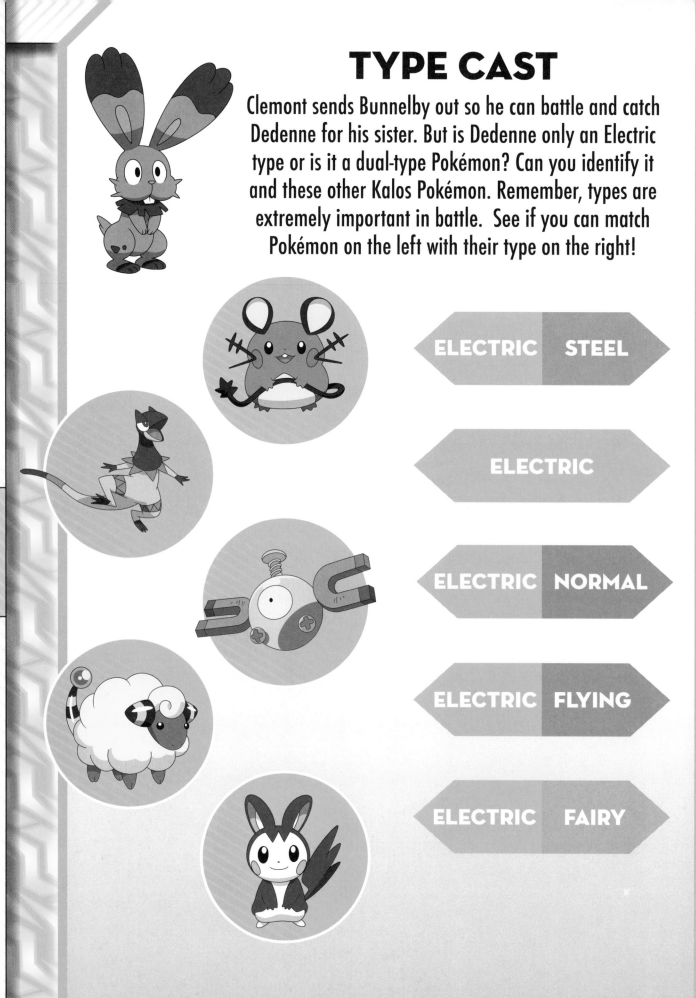

ELECTRIC STEEL

ELECTRIC

ELECTRIC NORMAL

ELECTRIC FLYING

ELECTRIC FAIRY

Turn to page 95 for the answers.

CLEMONT

SERENA & BONNIE

Serena and Bonnie aren't looking to train, exactly. Serena is a traveling companion because she remembers an act of kindness that a young Ash Ketchum bestowed upon her, and Bonnie is Clemont's younger sister. Their addition to the traveling party is key to Ash's success in Kalos!

COMPLETE THE TRAINER

So you've passed all the Specialist Training to become an expert in the Central, Coastal, and Mountain subregions of Kalos. Now let's see if you know the people you'll meet on your journey. Meet Serena—she has some history with Ash, but that history is a mystery! See if you can fill in the colors that Serena wears!

Turn to page 95 for the answer.

FIND THE DIFFERENCE

A good Kalos Pokémon Specialist knows how to spot a fake. Some of these Pokémon have a slight change in them—shape, appendages, color—and it's up to you and your sleuthing skills to find out which one is the real Pokémon!

A

B

C

D

Turn to page 95 for the answer.

COMPLETE BONNIE

Bonnie is Clemont's sister—and too young to be a Trainer.
But she'll do anything to be around Pokémon, and her
dedication to the Dedenne that her brother caught for her is adorable!!
See if you can fill in the colors that Bonnie wears!

Turn to page 95 for the answer.

PAPER SCRAWL

Bonnie spends all day scrawling Pokémon names in her notebook, because she dreams of one day becoming a Trainer. See if you can decipher her coded Pokémon names.

DIG ERZ BEE

SPU PAH

PIE ROR

HEEL EE OH LESK

NOY VER NN

BRRR GG MIGHT

CHEZ NOT

DA DEAN

Turn to page 95 for the answers.

CROSSWORD

You know your Pokémon, no doubt. Now let's see if you know about the human population of Kalos!

ACROSS

4. One of Professor Sycamore's assistants
5. He is the most famous Furfrou Groomer in Kalos
9. She upholds the law in Kalos (and everywhere else as well!)

DOWN

1. Alexa's sister, who happens to be a Gym Leader in Santalune City
2. Ash arrives in Kalos with this person but separates from her in Lumiose City
3. She is a Pokémon healer in Kalos (and everywhere else as well!)
5. The sister of 7 down
6. Her mom used to be a champion Rhyhorn racer
7. Bonnie's brother
8. She is Professor Sycamore's other assistant

Turn to page 95 for the answers.

TEAM ROCKET

They try, they really do. But no matter how nefarious their planning, Team Rocket always seems to lose their focus, and whatever prize they try to acquire. Where are they blasting off to in Kalos? Let's find out.

WHO'S YOUR FRIEND?

Team Rocket spends a lot of time trying to catch Pokémon—not necessarily their own, either! See if you can identify key Pokémon for Team Rocket from the list below.

Turn to page 95 for the answers.

SEEK AND FIND

Meowth is in hiding—along with other similar types!
That sneaky Team Rocket staple has camouflaged itself among other
Pokémon of the same type in the hopes that it won't get caught!

See if you can find it in this group of Pokémon. But wait—if you really
know the Pokémon of Kalos, pick out all Pokémon that are
the same type as Meowth. Types matter, Pokémon Specialists!

Turn to page 95 for the answers.

DOTS WHAT I'M TALKING ABOUT

Quick! James is trying to hide a Pokémon from Ash and his friends!
See if you can use the clues to identify this Pokémon.

CLUE 1:
It's a Dark and
Psychic type

CLUE 2:
The spots on its body
emit a flashing light

CLUE 3:
Eventually, it can evolve
into Malamar

If you guessed it in:
1 Clue: Your training is nearly complete!
2 Clues: You are really filling out your Pokédex!
3 Clues: I want you on my team!

Turn to page 95 for the answer.

A PUZZLE OF POKÉMON

Let's see if your identification skills have stayed sharp, Kalos Specialist!
Draw a line from the puzzle pieces to the missing spots in the puzzle.
Be careful! A wrong move might cost you your certificate!

A   **B**   **C**   **D**

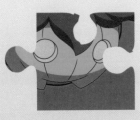

Turn to page 95 for the answers.

CRYPTO GRAPHICS

Professional Kalos Pokémon Specialists have been leaving coded messages all over the different subregions of Kalos looking for other specialists to talk to. But they've been replacing letters with Pokémon so that only the top specialists can decode them.

It prefers to ____ ____ ____ ____ in dark places, where its ____ ____ ____ ____ ____ tail can't be seen, and avoids battle when possible. If another Pokémon ____ ____ ____ ____ ____ ____ ____ it first, it puffs up its body and ____ ____ ____ ____ ____ ____ ____ back.

LEGEND

= A	= D	= I	= R
= B	= E	= K	= S
= C	= H	= L	= T

Turn to page 96 for the answers.

LEGENDARY & MEGA-EVOLVED POKÉMON

Well, friend, you have journeyed long and hard through Kalos,
and your reward is to witness some of the wonders of the land!
Welcome to the Legendary and Mega-Evolved Pokémon section, where you'll
meet not only the two X and Y namesakes, but Mega-Evolved Pokémon as well!

POKÉMON NAME GAME

Identifying your Pokémon before they disappear is very important to a Trainer. Here's a one-, two-, or multi-player word game that tests how quick you are at identifying Pokémon.

RULES

You and a friend pick out a Kalos Pokémon, like Xerneas. Each of you then writes that Pokémon's name down on a piece of paper. Now, come up with as many words as you can with the letters from that Pokémon name within a two-minute time limit. The player with the most words after two minutes wins.

Xerneas

1. An
2. Sane
3. Sea
4. Near
5. Ran
6. Rex
7. Earns
8. Snare
9. Ranees
10. Raxes

MEGA MAZE

You did it! You made it to one of the best kept secrets of Kalos! Follow Lucario deep into the maze and look for the Mega Stone, Lucarionite! Once you find the stone, push on to find the Mega Lucario!

START

FINISH

How does it feel to spot your first Mega-Evolved Pokémon? You are certainly on your way to fame and glory Pokémon Specialist!

Turn to page 96 for the answer.

WORD SCRAMBLE

Xerneas has a message for you. See if you can decipher what it's trying to say by taking the boxed letters from each clue and reassembling them into the words below!

1. One of three Legendary Pokémon that represent fire
LSTREMO _ ☐ _ _ _ ☐

2. They live in lightless caves and communicate with ultrasonic waves emitted from their ears.
INOTAB ☐ _ _ ☐ _ _

3. It can use its roots to control the trees around it to protect its forest home.
NTNTREAVE _ ☐ _ _ _ ☐ _ _ _

4. It loves to collect keys, and it will guard its collection with all its might.
IKLFKE _ ☐ ☐ _ _ ☐

5. The middle Evolution of Goomy
GOSLIGO ☐ _ _ _ _ ☐ _

6. The stone on top of its head can fire beams of energy.
BRIANCK _ _ ☐ ☐ _ _ _

7. It uses its whiskers like antennas to communicate.
DEENEND _ ☐ ☐ _ ☐ _ _

8. Its proficient fighting skills enable it to keep up with big bruisers like Machamp and Hariyama.
LUHHCWAA ☐ _ ☐ _ _ _ _ _

9. It often chases its own tail in a dizzying circle.
KITYST ☐ _ _ _ _ _

1. ☐☐ 2. ☐☐ 3. ☐☐ 4. ☐☐☐
5. ☐☐ 6. ☐☐ 7. ☐☐☐ 8. ☐☐ 9. ☐

ANSWER

Unscramble to reveal the message.
**Xerneas's _ _ _ _ _ shine in all the colors of the _ _ _ _ _ _ _ _.
It is said that this Legendary Pokémon can share the gift of _ _ _ _ _ _ _ _ life.**

Turn to page 96 for the answers.

MEGA MAZE

Lucario seemed pretty easy—so we're going to ramp up the challenge with one of the more fiery Pokémon. Follow Charizard deep into the maze and look for the Mega Stone, Charizardite X! Once you find the stone, push on to find the Mega Charizard X!

START

FINISH

Nicely done, Pokémon Specialist! You have managed to Mega-Evolve two Pokémon! Congratulations!

Turn to page 96 for the answer.

CRYPTO GRAPHICS

Professional Kalos Pokémon Specialists have been leaving coded messages all over the subregions of Kalos looking for other specialists to talk to. But they've been using Pokémon to replace letters so that only the top specialists can decode them.

Xerneas's type is _ _ _ _ _ and its weaknesses are _ _ _ _ _ and _ _ _ _ _ _ types.

LEGEND

= A	= I	= O	= S
= E	= L	= P	= T
= F	= N	= R	= Y

Turn to page 96 for the answers.

MEGA MAZE

You need to Mega-Evolve another Pokémon—this time, it's Mega Gengar! Follow Gengar through the maze, snag its Mega Stone, Gengarite, and work your way through the rest of the maze to Mega Gengar!

START

FINISH

You did it! That's three down – how many more are left?

Turn to page 96 for the answer.

FIND THE DIFFERENCE

A good Kalos Pokémon Specialist knows how to spot a fake. Some of these Pokémon have a slight change-shape, appendages, color—and it's up to you and your sleuthing skills to find out which one is the real Pokémon!

A

B

C

D

Turn to page 96 for the answer.

MEGA MAZE

The next Pokémon you need to Mega-Evolve is Absol.
This tough Pokémon is hard enough to catch in its regular form,
but now you have the chance to witness it as a Mega-Evolved
Pokémon once you've found its Mega Stone, Absolite!

START

FINISH

That should be
it for the Mega-Evolved . . . wait,
what? There's more?!?

Turn to page 96 for the answer.

POKÉMON ACROSTICS

You can play this fun game with one, two, or three players!

RULES

Pick a Pokémon name. Write that name in a column. If you picked Yveltal, you should have a puzzle that looks like this. Now, try to spell the longest word you can with the letters in each row. For example, starting with the first row, try to spell a word that starts with Y, but very long like YAWNED. You can only make one word per row, but you get one point for each letter used. Try for the longest word you know.

BONUS

Time the game, and see how many words you can come up with in two minutes.

yawned
V
E
L
T
A
L

MEGA MAZE

You may think you've found this Mega-Evolved Pokémon, but trust us, you haven't. Mega Charizard Y is slightly different, and it is completely ferocious! See if you can complete the search for the Charizardite Y Mega Stone and turn Charizard into Mega Charizard Y!

START

FINISH

Now you have seen both Mega Charizard X and Mega Charizard Y! Way to go!

Turn to page 96 for the answer.

CROSSWORD

Here's the final crossword, Pokémon Specialists!
See if you can answer this tough—and legendary—puzzle!

ACROSS

3. While some other Pokémon do this, Yveltal does not.
5. Yveltal is the _____ Pokémon.
8. This is one type for Yveltal.
9. Yveltal is weak against Electric-, Ice-, Fairy-, and _____ types.

DOWN

1. When Yveltal spreads its dark wings, its feathers give off a ____ glow.
2. The subregion of Kalos Yveltal belongs to.
4. This is Yveltal's other type.
6. It is said that Yveltal can absorb the life _____ of others.
7. Yveltal's gender is _____.

Turn to page 96 for the answers.

88

MEGA MAZE

You've made it Pokémon Specialist! The last of the
Mega Mazes for this adventure. Track down the Mega Blaziken
by following Blaziken's path to its Mega Stone, Blazikenite,
and then on to Mega-Evolved Blaziken! You can do it!

Turn to page 96 for the answer.

Certificate of Completion

You've correctly identified Pokémon from the Central, Coastal, and Mountain subregions of Kalos. Along the way you've met some Trainers traveling through Kalos along with their Pokémon. Finally, you've met some Legendary Pokémon and uncovered the mysteries of the Mega-Evolved Pokémon.

_____

has achieved the rank of Pokémon Specialist of the Kalos region.

XERNEAS

YVELTAL

MEGA BLAZIKEN

MEGA CHARIZARD X

MEGA ABSOL

MEGA GENGAR

Issued this _____ day of

_____, 20__

ANSWERS

If you've made it to the answer key, congratulations!
That means you have challenged yourself to become a true Pokemon Specialist
by completing your training activities. Good job! And if you're still in training,
then remember, only look at the answers for the training activities you've finished.

PAGE 6:

Height: 6'11"
Weight: 299.8 lbs.
Type(s): Fighting, Dark
Weaknesses: Flying, Fairy, Fighting
Unevolved Form: Pancham

PAGE 7:

D   B   A

PAGE 8:

Across and down crossword:
1. SHIELD
1(down). SCATTER
2(down). FLYING
3. THICKET
3(down). TETHER
4. EYES
5(down). STUB
6. PATTERNS
6(down). SEWPA
7. BUG
8(down). ROCK
9. GROUND

PAGE 9:

Word search containing: GOGOAT, FLETCHLING, BUNNELBY, SKIDDO, CHESPIN, VIVILLON, PYROAR, LITLEO, FURFROU

PAGE 10:

C — UNEVOLVED   A — 1ST EVOLUTION   B — 2ND EVOLUTION

Pokémon with two formes - Aegislash

PAGE 11:

Skiddo

PAGE 12:

PAGE 13:

L	W	R	X	S	I	I
1.	2.	3.	4.	5.	6.	7.

| S | W | I | R | L | I | X |

PAGE 14:

C

PAGE 15:

It **CONTROLS** the colony that **LIVES** in its honeycomb body by releasing **PHEROMONES**. It feeds the colony with honey provided by **COMBEE**.

PAGE 18:

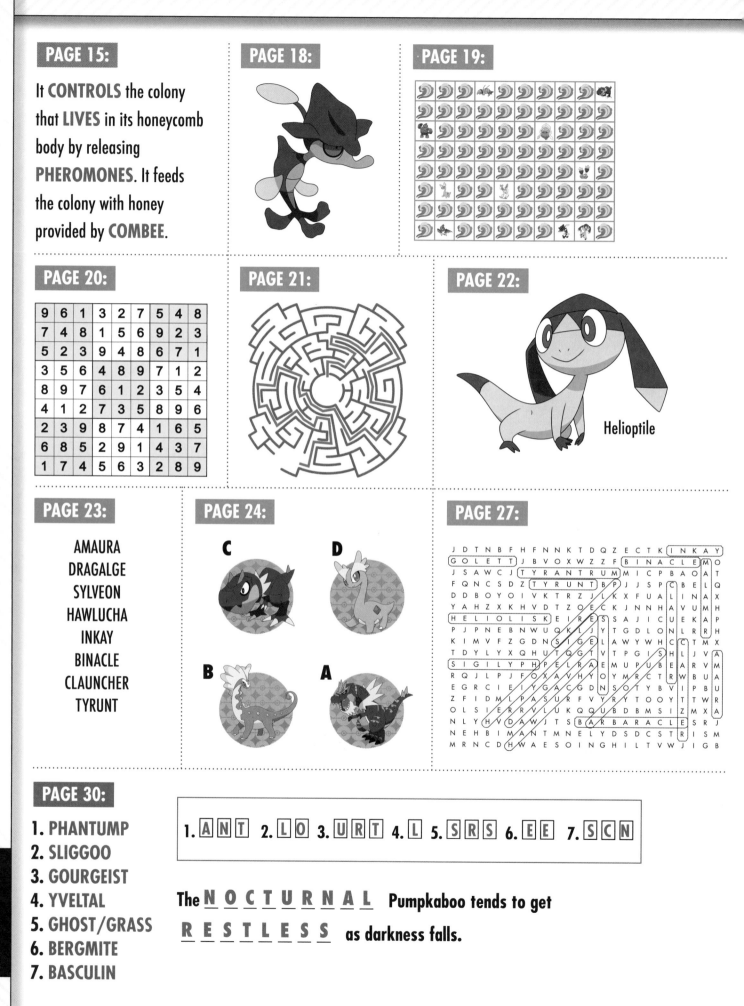

PAGE 19:

PAGE 20:

9	6	1	3	2	7	5	4	8
7	4	8	1	5	6	9	2	3
5	2	3	9	4	8	6	7	1
3	5	6	4	8	9	7	1	2
8	9	7	6	1	2	3	5	4
4	1	2	7	3	5	8	9	6
2	3	9	8	7	4	1	6	5
6	8	5	2	9	1	4	3	7
1	7	4	5	6	3	2	8	9

PAGE 21:

PAGE 22:

Helioptile

PAGE 23:

AMAURA
DRAGALGE
SYLVEON
HAWLUCHA
INKAY
BINACLE
CLAUNCHER
TYRUNT

PAGE 24:

C

D

B

A

PAGE 27:

PAGE 30:

1. PHANTUMP
2. SLIGGOO
3. GOURGEIST
4. YVELTAL
5. GHOST/GRASS
6. BERGMITE
7. BASCULIN

1. A N T   2. L O   3. U R T   4. L   5. S R S   6. E E   7. S C N

The N O C T U R N A L Pumpkaboo tends to get R E S T L E S S as darkness falls.

PAGE 31:

B

PAGE 32:

Suspects:

Klefki Gabite Noibat

Answer: Klefki

PAGE 33:

A B C

PAGE 34:

Basculin

PAGE 35:

GHOST GRASS

DRAGON

ICE

PAGE 36:

Gourgeist

PAGE 37:

1. M
2. MAGNETON
3. Y
4. MAGNEZONE
   M
   A
   G
   N
   E
   Z
   O
   N
   E
   Y
   R
   A
   N
   I
   T
   A
   R
6. MEWTWO
5. M
   U
   R
   K
   R
   O
   W
7. MAGNEMITE
8. MOWROTOM
9. MAGCARGO

PAGE 38:

PAGE 39:

A I X M H D J Y P T R P S V X N H M P E E Z
N M K F T K L E F K I H B O F Y Z A H I I I
S T Q W Z F I Z S P D A J S G Y O G V D U I
R B B Q O F I V T U B E V E Z S R O H I M M
F B A S C U L I N M U T D N K N O I V E R N
Q G V V A I G N M X U C K P R A M G P X E
G I W T Q S A P C K I M G O O D R A O N Z D
O N N R H L C R G R A W P Y T W X K L U B V M
O O N B E V R B I C H A B W J O Q Z O Z M U R E
M O N V A X L H O V O C N C N E F V W G R J W
Y J I T E A G O Y H O I J N Y C R P L E G T K
O A R N A R O M U Q E X S Z N E O Q I M E I C
Y F I A I C P E D H O N F W N L L J S G T I T
F K E N A X N P B K N Y C U Q F L B T E J M
Z P W T C U B C H O O X U N B U D C D E J M

PAGE 42:

PAGE 43:

Pikachu

Froakie

ANSWERS

93

PAGE 44:

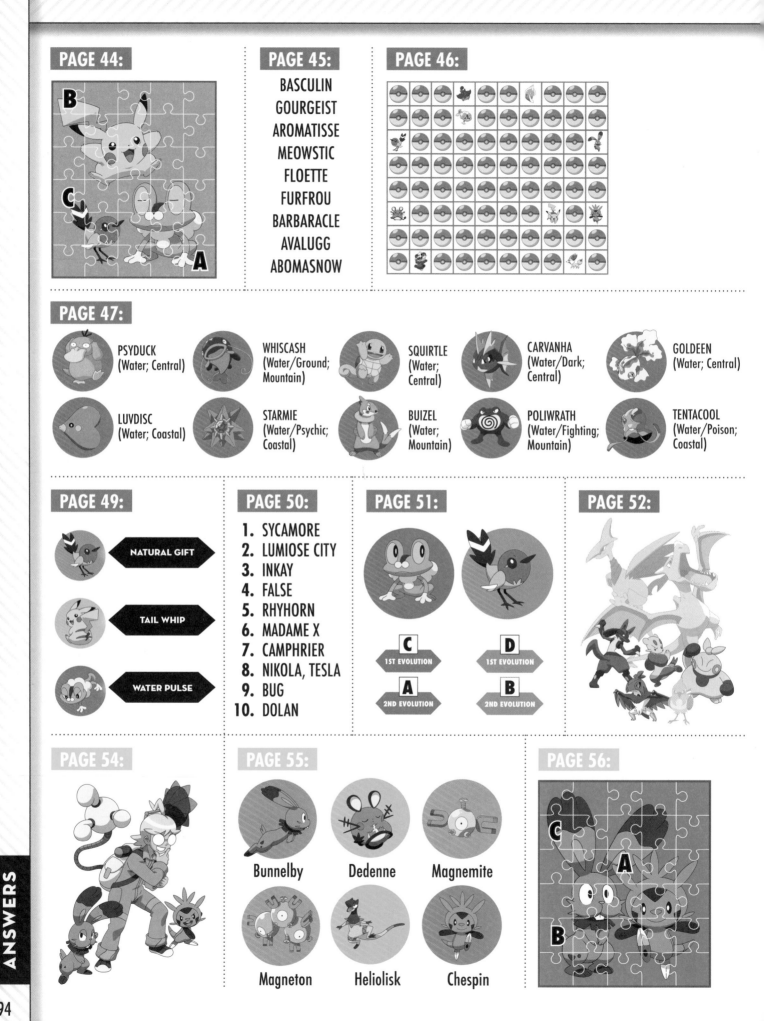

PAGE 45:

BASCULIN
GOURGEIST
AROMATISSE
MEOWSTIC
FLOETTE
FURFROU
BARBARACLE
AVALUGG
ABOMASNOW

PAGE 46:

PAGE 47:

PSYDUCK
(Water; Central)

WHISCASH
(Water/Ground;
Mountain)

SQUIRTLE
(Water;
Central)

CARVANHA
(Water/Dark;
Central)

GOLDEEN
(Water; Central)

LUVDISC
(Water; Coastal)

STARMIE
(Water/Psychic;
Coastal)

BUIZEL
(Water;
Mountain)

POLIWRATH
(Water/Fighting;
Mountain)

TENTACOOL
(Water/Poison;
Coastal)

PAGE 49:

NATURAL GIFT

TAIL WHIP

WATER PULSE

PAGE 50:

1. SYCAMORE
2. LUMIOSE CITY
3. INKAY
4. FALSE
5. RHYHORN
6. MADAME X
7. CAMPHRIER
8. NIKOLA, TESLA
9. BUG
10. DOLAN

PAGE 51:

C
1ST EVOLUTION

D
1ST EVOLUTION

A
2ND EVOLUTION

B
2ND EVOLUTION

PAGE 52:

PAGE 54:

PAGE 55:

Bunnelby

Dedenne

Magnemite

Magneton

Heliolisk

Chespin

PAGE 56:

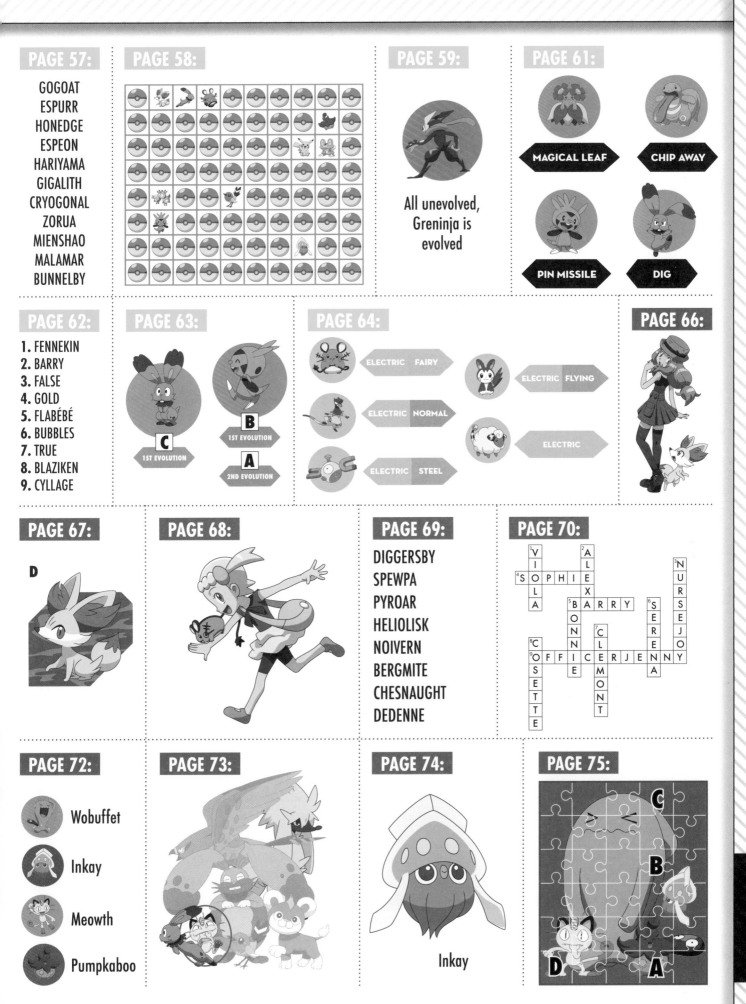

PAGE 57:

GOGOAT
ESPURR
HONEDGE
ESPEON
HARIYAMA
GIGALITH
CRYOGONAL
ZORUA
MIENSHAO
MALAMAR
BUNNELBY

PAGE 58:

PAGE 59:

All unevolved,
Greninja is
evolved

PAGE 61:

MAGICAL LEAF   CHIP AWAY

PIN MISSILE   DIG

PAGE 62:

1. FENNEKIN
2. BARRY
3. FALSE
4. GOLD
5. FLABÉBÉ
6. BUBBLES
7. TRUE
8. BLAZIKEN
9. CYLLAGE

PAGE 63:

C
1ST EVOLUTION

B
1ST EVOLUTION

A
2ND EVOLUTION

PAGE 64:

ELECTRIC   FAIRY

ELECTRIC   NORMAL

ELECTRIC   STEEL

ELECTRIC   FLYING

ELECTRIC

PAGE 66:

PAGE 67:

D

PAGE 68:

PAGE 69:

DIGGERSBY
SPEWPA
PYROAR
HELIOLISK
NOIVERN
BERGMITE
CHESNAUGHT
DEDENNE

PAGE 70:

Crossword:
- VIOLA
- ALEX
- NURSEJOY
- SOPHIE
- BONNIE
- BARRY
- SERENA
- CLEMONT
- COSETTE
- OFFICERJENNA

PAGE 72:

Wobuffet

Inkay

Meowth

Pumpkaboo

PAGE 73:

PAGE 74:

Inkay

PAGE 75:

C

B

D   A

PAGE 76:

It prefers to **HIDE** in dark places, where its **BLACK** tail can't be seen, and avoids battle when possible. If another Pokémon **ATTACKS** it first, it puffs up its body and **STRIKES** back.

PAGE 79:

PAGE 80:

1. MOLTRES
2. NOIBAT
3. TREVENANT
4. KLEFKI
5. SLIGGOO
6. CARBINK
7. DEDENNE
8. HAWLUCHA
9. SKITTY

1. O S   2. N A   3. R N   4. L E I
5. S O   6. R B   7. E D N   8. H W   9. S

Xerneas's **HORNS** shine in all the colors of the **RAINBOW**. It is said that this Legendary Pokémon can share the gift of **ENDLESS** life.

PAGE 81:

PAGE 82:

Xerneas's type is **FAIRY** and its weaknesses are **STEEL** and **POISON** types.

PAGE 83:

PAGE 84:

A

PAGE 85:

PAGE 87:

PAGE 88:

1. R (across) ³EVOLVE
2. M
MOUNTAIN
D
F
LYING
⁵D ⁶ESTRUCTION
N N
E K
⁸DARK N
G R
Y ⁹ROCK
N
N

PAGE 89: